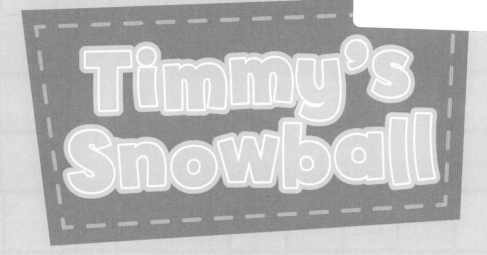

Timmy's Snowball

Adapted by
Benjamin Hulme-Cross

It was cold.

Timmy and Duck made a lot
of snowballs.

They had a snowball fight.

It got colder and colder.

Timmy went in.
He took a snowball with him.

Timmy put his snowball in a box.

Then he put a blanket on it.

Timmy had a nap.

Timmy got up.
He looked for his snowball.
It had melted!

"Where is my snowball?"
said Timmy.

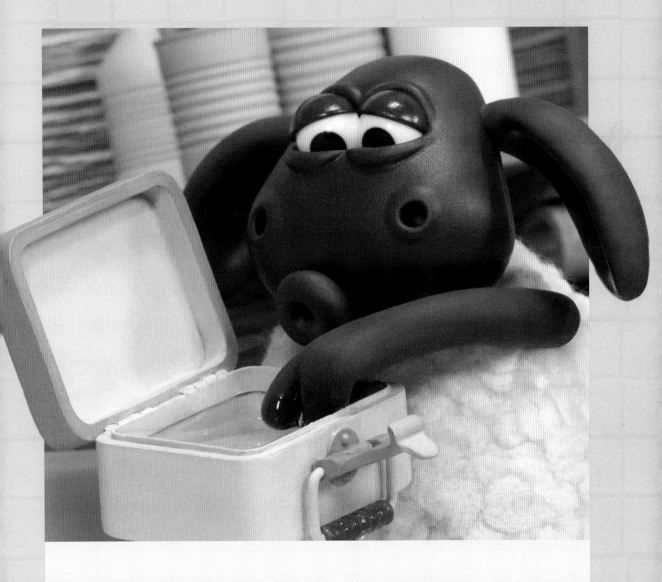

"The snowball has melted,"
Owl said.
"Snow needs to be cold."

"Wool snowballs will not melt!"
said Owl.

So Timmy made snowballs
with wool.